Almost My First Pet

Issomi Golden

WestBow Press books may be ordered through booksellers or by contacting:

WestBow Press
A Division of Thomas Nelson & Zondervan
1663 Liberty Drive
Bloomington, IN 47403
www.westbowpress.com
1 (866) 928-1240

This is a work of fiction. All of the characters, names, incidents, organizations, and dialogue in this novel are either the products of the author's imagination or are used fictitiously.

ISBN: 978-1-9736-6351-5 (sc)
ISBN: 978-1-9736-6352-2 (e)

Library of Congress Control Number: 2019906567

Print information available on the last page.

WestBow Press rev. date: 6/5/2019

WESTBOW
PRESS®
A DIVISION OF THOMAS NELSON
& ZONDERVAN

I would like to thank my husband, Terrance Golden, for believing in me and supporting me in my writing endeavors. He inspires me to keep going in life and to embrace my love of creating children's books.

DJ dreamed about having his very own pet. Almost every day for the past four months, DJ had asked his mom the same question: "Mommy, can I have a pet?"

His mom responded with the same answer each time: "What kind of pet would you like to have?"

DJ would reply with a crazy answer—a giraffe, a monkey, or even a snake. Of course, his mom would say no to each crazy animal he shouted out.

Finally, Mom said to DJ, "If you can say yes to these three questions, then that's the pet you can have."

Question number one: "Is the pet easy to take care of by yourself?"

Question number two: "Is the pet small enough to live inside the house?"

Question number three: "Is the pet safe enough to be around children?"

DJ walked away, thinking long and hard of what his first pet could possibly be.

Finally, he thought of the perfect pet: a goldfish. He was so excited. DJ imagined himself sitting in the kitchen and watching his goldfish swimming in a bowl. He ran to his mom with excitement. "Mommy, Mommy! I am finally ready for my first pet!"

His mom replied, "Are you sure? Pets can be a lot of work."

DJ said, "I'm ready, I'm ready!"

Mom then said, "Son, let's talk about this. If you still want your pet after we talk, you can have your pet."

Mom told DJ, "Pets take a lot of work. Every day, you have to put a leash on your pet and take it outside to use the bathroom. You have to do this first thing in the morning and every evening when you get home from school, no matter how tired you are. We do not want your pet having a bathroom accident inside."

DJ imagined putting a leash on his goldfish so that it could use the bathroom outside. He thought, *I do not want Mommy to get mad at me because my goldfish went to the bathroom inside.*

DJ's mom continued. "You also have to make sure your pet is strong and healthy. So you will need to make sure you feed it every day. It is important not to forget to give it dog food because it may start to eat other things, like the furniture or my favorite pair of shoes."

DJ began to imagine feeding his goldfish dog food. He thought it was odd to feed a fish dog food, but he wanted to make sure he did everything his mom told him to.

Next, Mom told DJ, "Your pet will get stinky. You will have to bathe it with soap and water at least once a month. If you don't, then it will make the house smell bad."

DJ began to imagine himself doing exactly what his mother told him to. He had to wash his goldfish with soap and water. Although it was odd, he did not want the house to stink because he had a dirty fish.

DJ's mom said, "Most pets love to play ball. These pets will play all day if you let them. It is important to play ball with your pet so it can stay active. This will make it sleep better at night."

DJ imagined playing ball with his goldfish. At first, he wasn't sure how to do this while his fish was in the fishbowl, so he pictured taking it outside and putting it on the ground. Although it was odd that a fish would like to play catch with a ball, DJ wanted to do everything his mom said.

DJ asked his mom, "What other rules are there for taking care of my first pet?"

She replied, "You will need to comb and brush your pet every other day. The more you brush your pet's hair, the less hair it will shed around the house. Too much pet hair lying around the house will make Mommy sneeze."

DJ imagined brushing his goldfish with a brush so his mom would not sneeze. *That sure is strange, brushing my goldfish when it doesn't have any hair,* DJ thought.

Mom said, "Sometimes it will be cold and raining outside. You will still need to take your pet outside every day to use the bathroom. To keep pets warm and dry, some people dress up their pets."

DJ imagined trying to put a pair of pants on his goldfish. He thought, *My goldfish doesn't have any legs; how will it be able to put on these pants?*

DJ had all these crazy thoughts going through his head. *I know my fish will need fresh air, and it will have to learn how to use the bathroom outside. Mommy just told me that she does not want my pet to use the bathroom inside the house. I wonder if I can take my fish outside on nice sunny days with no clothes on. I can take it into the backyard, where no one can see that it is naked. I will train it to use the bathroom really quickly and take it back inside before anyone sees us.*

DJ also thought, *I have to brush my teeth every day. Sometimes two times, when Mommy catches me before I get in bed to go to sleep. I'm sure Mommy will tell me to brush my pet's teeth. I need to learn to do things for my first pet without her always having to tell me to do them. Do goldfish even have teeth? I hope it is not allergic to my toothpaste. I wonder if there is fish toothpaste that I can buy from the store.*

DJ's imagination had given him a lot of questions to ask.

Mom then told DJ that she had found an old collar that had the name Spike on it. She asked him if he could name his first pet Spike so that his pet could wear the collar.

DJ remembered his teacher telling one of his schoolmates that it was important that every pet wear a name tag. If a pet got lost, the people who found it would know how to contact the owner.

This is perfect, DJ thought. *I already have a name for my fish.*

DJ began to imagine his fish swimming in a bowl wearing the collar that had the name Spike written on the side. DJ thought, *This is really weird. I don't think my fish will be able to swim with a big collar around him. He doesn't even have a neck.*

DJ then said to his mom, "Taking care of pets is too hard. Having to walk, play ball, clean, and feed my pet dog food every day is too much work for a fish. Mommy, I changed my mind. I do not want a pet."

Mom was surprised at what DJ said to her. "A fish? A fish is what you want to have as your first pet? That's what you should have said in the beginning, son. I thought you wanted a dog for your first pet."

DJ was tired of imagining performing all these chores for a pet that he didn't even have. He looked at his mom and said, "Never mind, Mom. I don't want a pet."

CPSIA information can be obtained
at www.ICGtesting.com
Printed in the USA
BVHW020029180619
551189BV00042B/2740/P

9 781973 663515